Surprise! Surprise!

For John Salmon,
who really did surprise his mum.

Copyright © 1995 by Michael Foreman
This paperback edition first published in 2004 by Andersen Press Ltd.
The rights of Michael Foreman to be identified as the author and illustrator of this work have been asserted by
him in accordance with the Copyright, Designs and Patents Act, 1988. First published in Great Britain in 1995 by
Andersen Press Ltd., 20 Vauxhall Bridge Road, London SW1V 2SA. Published in Australia by Random House
Australia Pty., 20 Alfred Street, Milsons Point, Sydney, NSW 2061. Colour separated in Switzerland
by Photolitho AG, Zürich. Printed and bound in Italy by Grafiche AZ, Verona.

10 9 8 7 6 5 4 3 2 1

British Library Cataloguing in Publication Data available.

ISBN 1 84270 379 X

This book has been printed on acid-free paper

Surprise! Surprise!

Written and illustrated by
Michael Foreman

Andersen Press • London

Mum finished the story and kissed Little Panda goodnight.
Little Panda snuggled down in his bed and went to sleep
in the glow of his Moonlight.

He loved his Moonlight. It kept the dark away and Little Panda was frightened of the dark.

The next night it was Dad's turn to read. When he finished
the story he kissed Little Panda goodnight. Then he said, "It's
Mum's birthday soon. What will you give her for a present?"
"A surprise," said Little Panda.

The next day, Little Panda opened his piggy bank. He found two chocolate buttons, a bottle top and a shiny silver coin. He sucked the chocolate buttons while he wondered what he could buy with a bottle top and a shiny silver coin.

He went to the shop.
"May I have the biggest plant I can get for this shiny silver coin, please," said Little Panda.

The shopkeeper looked at Little Panda's money and gave him a tiny plant in a pot. "It's very small," said Little Panda. "So is your coin," said the shopkeeper.

The plant was so tiny that Little Panda was able to take it home without his mum noticing.

Although he hated to go there, he hid it in the attic, as he knew it was the only place his mum wouldn't look.

Ooooh ... spooky! It was so dark.

Little Panda wanted to run back downstairs, but he knew he must be brave. He took a deep breath and read the label on the pot.
'This plant likes plenty of water and sunlight.'

Little Panda gave the plant a drink from the big water tank, and then he had an idea . . . he didn't know how to give the plant sunlight, but he did have his Moonlight.

That night, after Mum and Dad had kissed him goodnight, Little Panda crept out of bed and took his Moonlight to the attic.

The attic was even more spooky at night than in the day. Little Panda thought the plant would be happier with his Moonlight.

Little Panda's room was now even darker than the attic, but he was brave. The tiny plant needed the Moonlight more than he did.

In the morning he got the Moonlight from the attic and put it back beside his bed before Mum called him for breakfast.

Every night, Little Panda gave the plant a drink and his Moonlight. Soon, he got used to the dark and didn't find it frightening any more.

At last it was Mum's birthday.

Little Panda waited while Mum had breakfast in bed. He waited and waited while Mum opened her present from Dad. He waited and waited and waited while Mum opened all her birthday cards.

Then Little Panda said, "Follow me!"
His mum and dad followed him upstairs,
and Little Panda opened the door to the attic!